Table of Contents

R0429302619

RICKY VARGAS:
Born to Be Funny!

by Alan Katz
with illustrations by Stacy Curtis

Scholastic I...

RICKY VARGAS:

Born to Be Funny!

To Rachel and Jordan, two of the funniest and sweetest kids I know.
—A. K.

For the funny Francis family, thanks for the laughs!
—S. C.

No part of this publication may be reproduced, stored in a retrieval system, or transmitted in any form or by any means, electronic, mechanical, photocopying, recording, or otherwise, without written permission of the publisher. For information regarding permission, write to Scholastic Inc., Attention: Permissions Department, 557 Broadway, New York, NY 10012.

Text copyright © 2012 by Alan Katz.
Illustrations copyright © 2012 by Scholastic Inc.

Illustrations by Stacy Curtis.
All rights reserved. Published by Scholastic Inc.
SCHOLASTIC and associated logos are trademarks and/or registered trademarks of Scholastic Inc.

Library of Congress Cataloging-in-Publication Data is available.

ISBN 978-0-545-31396-4

10 9 8 7 6 5 4 3 2 1   13 14 15 16 17

Printed in the U.S.A.   40
This edition first printing, February 2013

The Unfunny Day Story

Everyone who has ever met Ricky Vargas says he's the funniest kid in the world.

His mom says so. His dad says so.
So does his violin teacher, his
mailman, his baseball coach,
and his aunt Jen.

Now, of course, those people haven't met *all the other* kids in the world, so there *may* be a funnier kid somewhere.

But if so, they haven't met him.

Or her.

Ricky does funny things.

Ricky says funny things.

And just by being himself,

he's made people's lives happier

for all 2,704 days he's been alive.

Until today.

See, when Ricky woke up this
morning, Ricky felt *funny*...
because he didn't feel funny.

He got dressed in very
serious clothes.

He ate a very serious breakfast.

14

And he had a very serious chat
with his parents.

Ricky's mom felt his head.

Ricky's dad looked in his throat.

But it was clear Ricky wasn't sick—
he just wasn't funny.

And in the classroom,

when Mrs. Wilder asked,

Ricky didn't say, "All of them," to make everyone laugh.

Ricky wasn't funny
at recess. Or at lunch.
Or anywhere.

His buddy Eddie did his
best to help.

And it made everyone say...

It was weird, but when the funniest kid stopped being funny, everyone else stopped laughing.

Good thing Eddie came up
with a plan.

He said, "Maybe if we make
Ricky laugh, he'll start making
us laugh again!"

22

The rest of the day, everyone
tried to make Ricky laugh.

His teacher tried.
His friends tried.
Even his principal tried.

Just before the end of this
very serious day, it was
time for science.

Mrs. Wilder showed the
class how sliced onion
makes most people cry.

She sliced...and everyone cried.

Everyone
except
Ricky.

He just laughed. And laughed.
And laughed and laughed
and laughed. He giggled.
And even snorted once or twice.

28

And even though they were crying, Ricky's teacher and friends were happy, because they could tell that tomorrow...

...Ricky Vargas would be the funniest kid in the world once again!

The Talent Contest Story

The sign-up sheet for the school
talent contest was up on
the board.

Twenty-seven kids had entered.
But no one expected to win.

No one except Ricky Vargas,
the funniest kid in the world.

Hannah Smith signed up
because her mother told her to.

But Hannah was so sure she'd lose that she only brought one tap shoe.

Twins Lee and Paul Baron
joined the contest,
but didn't really agree on
what they would be singing.

Even The Amazing Alvin changed his name.

Because let's face it, when you're up against the funniest kid in the world, there's no chance you are going to win a talent contest.

The contest was going to
take place right after school.
So that whole day, everyone
was thinking about it.

Especially Ricky.

Warming up for the contest, Ricky was very funny in class.

Hello, I am Ricky Alva Edison, inventor of the Frontpack.

Ricky was extra
funny in the library.

And Ricky was wildly funny at lunch, acting like the food on everyone's trays.

Everywhere Ricky went,
he had everyone laughing
all day.

Finally it was four o'clock, and
the whole school was waiting
for the talent contest to begin.

Mrs. Wilder was the host of the show. She told everyone to have a good time.

TAP!

THUNK!

TAP!

THUNK!

The crowd cheered each performer, no matter how good, bad, or odd they were.

49

After almost an hour, there were just two performers left.

Timmy Thomas played "Happy Birthday" very well.

Then Ricky did all his best bits...
the ones that had been so funny
earlier in the day.

But since everyone had already
seen them all, this time no one
laughed.

And when the judges added up
their scores, the winner was...

...Timmy, for playing "Yankee Doodle" on the tuba.

54

Ricky was glad for Timmy. And he learned an important lesson that day–

The Substitute Teacher Story

Second grade was full of
surprises. But the one thing
Ricky Vargas could always
count on was...

...that Mrs. Wilder would show up for class each and every day.

Ricky loved seeing her
smiling face, and he loved
making her laugh.

Welcome Class!

So it was a shock when
Ricky got to class and saw
a different teacher sitting
at Mrs. Wilder's desk.

Ricky's head went "Boing!"
Ricky's heart went "Boing!"
And Ricky's pencil box went
"Boing!"—because he dropped
it on the floor.

The teacher said her name was
Mrs. Adams, and that since
Mrs. Wilder was sick,
she would be taking over the
class that day.

Ricky was worried.
About Mrs. Wilder.
And about the class.

About an hour later,
Ricky knew he was right
to have been worried.

Mrs. Adams had them do a lot
of work. A lot.

And while there's nothing wrong with working hard, Ricky had a big problem. See, the teacher was...

...serious.

Very serious.

Very, very, very serious.

Ricky figured she went to
Mean College, where she studied
Mean Math, Mean Science, and
Mean History.

Mrs. Adams seemed to get meaner
each time Ricky tried to make
her smile.

She didn't like it when
he got the whole class
to switch seats while
her back was turned.

Or when he sharpened
his carrot stick.

Or when he solved the math
problem by meowing the answer.

Mrs. Adams sent Ricky to the principal's office twice. He also had to write three "I'm sorry" notes.

All for being his usual funny self.

Ricky learned a lot of math, science, and history that day.

But he also learned something else.
Something far more important.

He learned that there is a right time and a right place to be funny. And that if you run into someone who doesn't want to laugh, that's the time to be serious.

Ricky hoped Mrs. Wilder would
be back soon.

But somehow, he was glad he'd
met Mrs. Adams.

Even if she was very serious.

How to Be the Funniest Kid in the World

Ricky, if I have 20 nickels in my left pocket, and 25 dimes in my right pocket, what does that make?

A lot of noise!

Ricky, this cotton candy doesn't taste right!

That's odd, I made it with real cotton!

The gym teacher told us to take a one-mile run or a two-lap swim.

What are you going to take?

A three-hour nap!

Ricky, why did you give me these sunglasses?

Yesterday you told me I'm a very bright student.

GET MORE OF
RICKY VARGAS,
THE FUNNIEST KID IN THE WORLD!

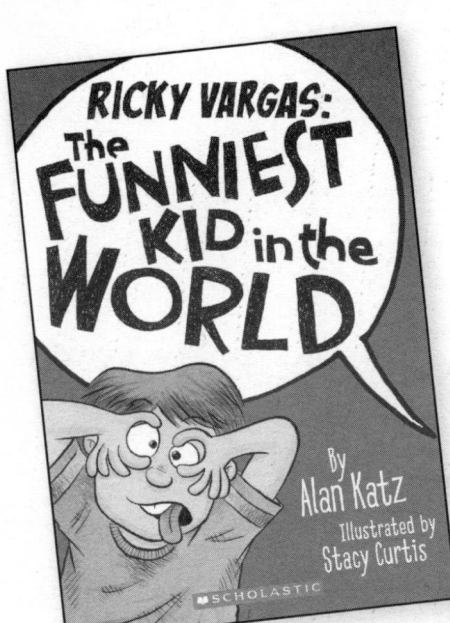

Available in print
and eBook editions

■SCHOLASTIC
scholastic.com

VARGASe